The Wonky Donkey

For my mum,
and all the people who have helped me
over the years: family, friends and mentors.
Thank you.
– Craig Smith

To my precious Mum, Dad and Aunt Wren ...
your love, support and inspiration fuels my creative journey
and makes all of me smile and sing. With big-fat gratitude
for keeping me tuned to the magic and humour of life.
– Katz Cowley

ISBN 978-0-545-26124-1

Published by Scholastic Inc. SCHOLASTIC and associated logos are trademarks and/or registered trademarks of Scholastic Inc.

Library of Congress Cataloging-in-Publication Data Available

18 17 16   18 19 20/0
Printed in the U.S.A.   76

This edition first printing, May 2010

The artwork was created using watercolors.
The text was set in Drawzing Regular
Book design by Book Design Ltd, Christchurch, www.bookdesign.co.nz

The Wonky Donkey

Words and music by Craig Smith

Illustrations by Katz Cowley

SCHOLASTIC INC.

NEW YORK TORONTO LONDON AUCKLAND
SYDNEY MEXICO CITY NEW DELHI HONG KONG

I was walking down the road
and I saw ...

a donkey,

Hee Haw!

And he only had three legs!

He was a
wonky donkey.

I was walking down the road
and I saw a donkey,

Hee Haw!

He only had three legs ...

and one eye!

He was a **winky** wonky donkey.

I was walking down the road
and I saw a donkey,

Hee Haw!

He only had three legs,
one eye ...

and he liked to listen to country music.

Yee Haw!

He was a **honky-tonky**
winky wonky donkey.

I was walking down the road
and I saw a donkey,

Hee Haw!

He only had three legs,
one eye,
he liked to listen to country music ...

and he was quite tall and slim.

He was a **lanky** honky-tonky winky wonky donkey.

I was walking down the road
and I saw a donkey,

Hee Haw!

He only had three legs,
one eye,
he liked to listen to country music,
he was quite tall and slim ...

and he smelt really, really bad.

He was a **stinky-dinky**
lanky honky-tonky
winky wonky donkey.

I was walking down the road
and I saw a donkey,

Hee Haw!

He only had three legs,
one eye,
he liked to listen to country music,
he was quite tall and slim,
he smelt really, really bad ...

**and that morning he'd got up early
and hadn't had any coffee.**

He was a cranky
stinky-dinky lanky
honky-tonky
winky wonky donkey.

I was walking down the road
and I saw a donkey,

Hee Haw!

He only had three legs,
one eye,
he liked to listen to country music,
he was quite tall and slim,
he smelt really, really bad,
that morning he'd got up early
and hadn't had any coffee ...

and he was always getting up to mischief.

He was a **hanky-panky** cranky stinky-dinky lanky honky-tonky winky wonky donkey.

I was walking down the road
and I saw a donkey,

Hee Haw!

He only had three legs,
one eye,
he liked to listen to country music,
he was quite tall and slim,
he smelt really, really bad,
that morning he'd got up early
and hadn't had any coffee,
he was always getting up to mischief ...

but he was quite good looking!

He was a **spunky** hanky-panky cranky
stinky-dinky lanky honky-tonky winky wonky donkey!

I was walking down the road

and I saw a donkey ...

Hee Haw!